Under The Leaf

Written by Jill Eggleton
Illustrated by Richard Hoit

Rigby

"I am hot,"
said Monkey.

Monkey went under
a **big** leaf.

"I am hot, too,"
said Lion.

"Come under the leaf,"
said Monkey.

"I am hot, too,"
said Tiger.

"Come under the leaf,"
said Lion.

bzz z z z z z

The mosquito looked
at Monkey and Lion
and Tiger.

8

The mosquito went bzzzzzz up to the leaf.

The mosquito went bzzzzzz on Lion.

"**Ouch!**" said Lion.

The mosquito went bzzzzzz
on Tiger.
"**Ouch!**" said Tiger.

The mosquito went bzzzzzz
on Monkey.
"Ouch! Ouch! Ouch!"
said Monkey.

13

The mosquito went under the big leaf!

A Story Sequence

1

2

3

4

15

Guide Notes

Title: Under the Leaf
Stage: Early (1) – Red

Genre: Fiction
Approach: Guided Reading
Processes: Thinking Critically, Exploring Language, Processing Information
Written and Visual Focus: Cumulative Sequence Panel, Story Sequence

THINKING CRITICALLY
(sample questions)
- What do you think this story could be about?
- Look at the title and read it to the children.
- Why do you think the animals were hot?
- How do you know the animals did not like the mosquito?
- Why do you think the mosquito did what he did to the animals?
- How do you know the animals were nice to each other?
- What do you think the animals did when they left the big leaf?

EXPLORING LANGUAGE

Terminology
Title, cover, illustrations, author, illustrator

Vocabulary
Interest words: ouch, buzz
High-frequency words: too, up, looked
Positional words: up, under, on

Print Conventions
Capital letter for sentence beginnings and names (**M**onkey, **L**ion, **T**iger), periods, commas, quotation marks, exclamation marks